Get well SOON!

SMILE!

courage

STAY strong

*To Mum and Dad, for everything.*

I want to extend my gratitude to everyone at Allen and Unwin, especially to my wonderful editor
Nicola Santilli for her unwavering support, guidance and enthusiasm, and my publisher Anna McFarlane for
entrusting me with this special project and helping me achieve my dream of publishing my first picture book.
Thank you also to designer extraordinaire, Sandra Nobes, who had the tough job of putting everything together
and working her magic to make my art and text come alive. I'm so lucky my first book was in your hands!

Thank you to the ever-patient health professionals who lent me invaluable knowledge in the research
of this book. Thank you to Dr Eugene Moylan, Dr Paul Chay and the Liverpool Paediatric Team for not only sharing
your wisdom and knowledge in your fields of expertise, but also taking the time to guide me through Liverpool Hospital's
paediatric ward and emergency department. A big shout-out to Mary-Kate Moylan for providing feedback on my
drafts and answering a gazillion questions about the emergency department. A giant nod to Jonathan Young for your
insights into physiotherapy. A huge thank you to Dr Frances Yuen for sharing your experience working at
children's hospitals, providing varied guidance, and showing me the great lengths to which hospital workers
help make hospitals a warm and positive place for sick children.

My gratitude towards disability sensitivity reader Jessica Walton for providing feedback to ensure my book
was as inclusive for all children as possible.

To my friends and family – thank you for always supporting me, particularly my mum who nurtured my love for
art from the moment I picked up a crayon. Lastly, thank you to my partner Luke, for being my rock.

Without you all, this book would not have been possible.

# A Trip TO THE HOSPITAL

## FREDA CHIU

ALLEN&UNWIN

SYDNEY · MELBOURNE · AUCKLAND · LONDON

First published by Allen & Unwin in 2021

Allen & Unwin
83 Alexander Street
Crows Nest NSW 2065
Australia
Phone: (61 2) 8425 0100
Email: info@allenandunwin.com
Web: www.allenandunwin.com

A catalogue record for this book is available from the National Library of Australia

ISBN 978 1 76052 670 2

For teaching resources, explore www.allenandunwin.com/resources/for-teachers

Illustration technique: mixed media and digital artwork

Cover design by Freda Chiu and Sandra Nobes
Internal design by Sandra Nobes
Set in Camping Holiday and Chewy Caramel
This book was printed in June 2022 by Hang Tai Printing Company Limited, China

3 5 7 9 10 8 6 4 2

MIX
Paper from responsible sources
FSC® C023121

www.fredachiu.com

RANI HENRY MOMO

# Introducing . . . our SUPERHEROES!

MATEO
Nurse

FRANCES
Paediatrician

EUGENE
Oncologist

FATIMA
Radiographer

SOO-MIN
Surgeon

JACK — Porter

KIRRA — Paramedic

ANNA — Anaesthetist

JONNY — Physiotherapist

ROSIE — Cleaner

These are some of the people who will help you feel better. They might be wearing funny masks, gowns and hats, but underneath . . .

They're just like YOU!

Before you enter the hospital,
there are some rules you must follow.

'May I ask you some questions?'

'Please wash your hands.'

'Let me take your temperature.'

# You might be expected

## or be a surprise.

No matter how you arrive, we are always prepared.

Once you're inside, sometimes you must wait.

TRIAGE 1

If you arrive through
the emergency department,
a triage nurse will ask
how you feel...

...to make sure the sickest people are seen first.

When it's your turn, someone will call your name.

Henry?

Rani?

People go to hospital for all sorts of reasons and treatments.

It's a
**BIG**
place

filled with shiny machines,
clever people and lots of activity.

Momo has asthma and is having trouble breathing. Nurse Mateo does some tests to make sure her body is working properly and to give her the right treatment.

HEIGHT and WEIGHT

OXYGEN LEVELS

Using tiny light beams, this painless device says if Momo is getting enough oxygen into her body.

TEMPERATURE

BREATHING

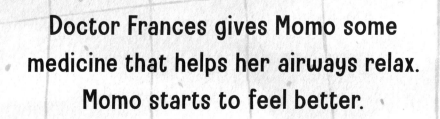

Doctor Frances gives Momo some
medicine that helps her airways relax.
Momo starts to feel better.

Last year, Henry came to hospital
for medicine to treat bone cancer,
a disease that made him very sick.

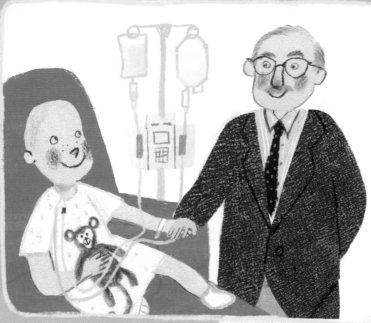

Last month, he got a shiny new leg.
Henry likes to think he is
part robot!

Today, Jonny the
physiotherapist is helping
Henry make his muscles strong.

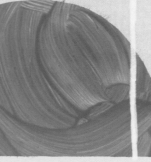

Henry does lots of exercises.
Sometimes they are hard,
but he gets better and
better every week.

Henry wants to be
a basketball player one day.

Rani hurt her arm.
Fatima the radiographer uses the
X-ray machine to take a photo
of her bones.

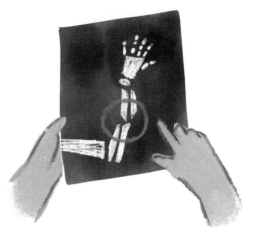

Rani needs an operation!
Doctor Soo-min the surgeon explains everything that will happen.

You won't
feel a thing!

Doctor Anna the anaesthetist will give Rani
a special medicine to keep her asleep the whole time.

Jack the porter wheels Rani into another room...

. . . and Rani falls fast asleep.

After an operation, you will wake up in a recovery room
with a nurse taking care of you.

When you feel better, you might be taken to a ward to rest or you might be allowed to go home.

Sometimes you can
go to the playroom.

Sometimes the playroom
comes to you!

Hospital school is just around the corner.
If you stay in hospital for a long time,
you are always welcome.

Even if you are in bed!

It's time to go home.

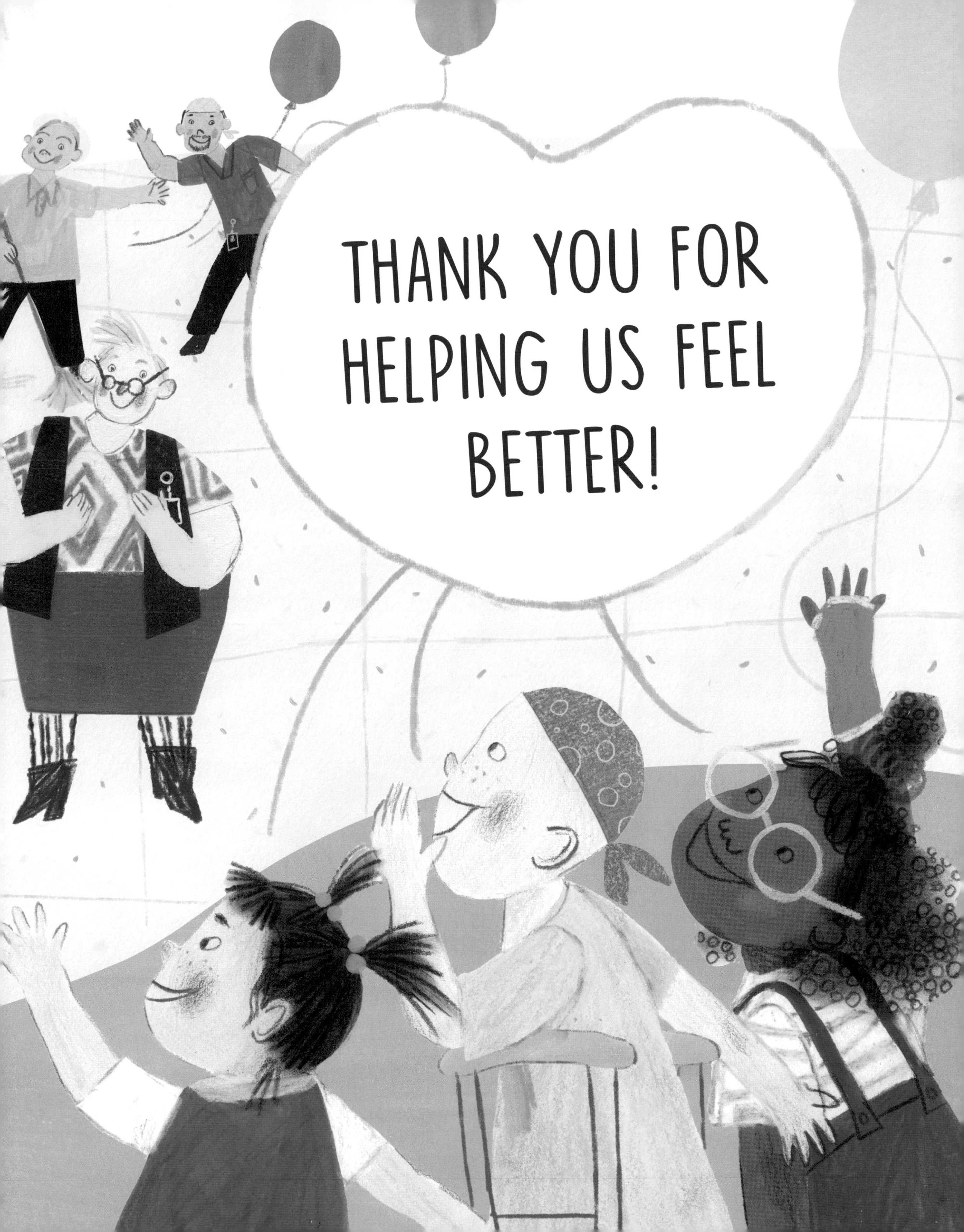
THANK YOU FOR HELPING US FEEL BETTER!

Goodbye!

# Did You Know?

Australia's first children's hospital opened in Melbourne in 1870 with just six rooms. Wow!

All over the world, clown doctors visit sick kids in hospitals to give
them the best kind of medicine – laughter!

When you come through hospital emergency, you will be allocated a triage category based
on how quickly you need help: immediately, or within 10 minutes, 30 minutes, 1 hour or 2 hours.
This makes sure the sickest people are seen first.

Australian hospital worker uniforms are colour-coded. Can you spot the difference
between doctors, nurses, physiotherapists and cleaners?

Australian doctors and scientists have invented many helpful things:
Spray-on skin!  ○  A bionic eye!  ○  The electronic pacemaker!
The bionic ear/cochlear implant!  ○  The world's first anti-cancer vaccine!

Many people helped with the research for this book.
Some are even illustrated as characters! Who can you find?

JONNY

FRANCES

EUGENE

PAUL

MARY-KATE